DEATH OF THE SWAN

By

Sophie Storm-Henningsen

Table of Contents

Table of Contents

To anyone who's ever felt out of place

Acknowledgment

First of all, I would like to thank my family. I wouldn't have been able to finish this novel without your support.

I would also like to mention my friends, Henriette, Ena, Signe, Maja, Ida, and Emma. Without your help and guidance, I would never have been able to write this book. Thank you for being so overbearing and reading through every draft I sent. You helped me find my way.

Of course, I need to thank my team of editors. You have helped me navigate in the business of self-publishing, and I couldn't have done it without you.

As the majority of this book has been written during my hospitalization, A special thank you go out to the nurses of P50 at Odense University hospital (the Psychiatric ward). You helped me see that my illness doesn't define me, and even though I may have obstacles and challenges to overcome, anything is possible.

Last, but not least; thank you to the readers! This book wouldn't be possible if it weren't for you. You have my most sincere thanks.

About the Author

Sophie was born in Odense, Denmark in 2001. She is currently studying American Studies at the Southern University of Denmark and will graduate with her bachelor's degree in the summer of 2025.

She lives with her best friend in a studio apartment in Odense, Denmark, and intends on continuing her studies, following her graduation.

This is her debut novel.

Chapter 1

I was 6 years old when I first fantasized about killing Mother. We had just returned home from ballet class, and she had, as usual, pointed out all my mistakes in front of everyone. I knew I was better than everyone in that class, but it seemed as if Mother refused to see how brilliant I was when I danced and only focused on the terrible aspects of my learning years. The familiar smell of cigarettes and old wine felt like a wall whenever I entered the house. Even though I was used to it by now, my face still scrunched up at the stench. The verbal beating continued as I followed her through the house.

"It is so simple, Catherine! How can you not count to four!?" Mother yelled as I kept my head down and waited.

"I taught you better than that! I cannot believe you!"

"I'm trying," I whispered, knowing it would only get worse if I crossed her.

"That's what you call trying?!"

"…yes," I said hesitantly to the floor, refusing to meet her eye.

"I'm going to sit in the living room, and if I see you before I call your name, I swear to God, Catherine!!" Her arms waved around her, forming into fists as she said my name. I saw the rage in her eyes, and I knew what was coming if I didn't do as I was told. A beating would follow. I was used to it, but instead of provoking her anymore, I went upstairs and closed my bedroom door. I never bothered to cry about Mother, as she rarely was correct in her arguments and opinions about my dancing. I knew I was amazing, and if I kept working hard, I would become the best dancer the world had ever seen.

As I began to grow hungry but hadn't heard my name being called, I sneaked a peak through my door. Silence. I ventured silently and slowly out of my room (still in my outfit from ballet class) and tip-toed down the stairs, carefully avoiding the fourth and seventh steps that creaked when stepped on. As I reached the end of the staircase, I could hear Mother's deep breathing. She had fallen asleep. Around her was a heavy cloud of smoke that had spread throughout the entire living room and slowly made its way toward the kitchen. I quickly, and as silently as I could manage, ran to the kitchen door and shut it before any more smoke could enter. I covered my face with my elbow and squinted my eyes as I walked back toward the living room to ensure Mother was still breathing. As I peeked into the room from the hallway and removed my arm from my face, I saw Mother asleep in her brown leather chair. A lit cigarette was in her hand, and her neck was exposed. It was then that the fantasy of strangling her with my small but strong arms first came to mind. I visualized through burning eyes how I would see the life leave her eyes as I ripped the tendons from her throat.

Instead, I went over to her with a smile on my face and put out her cigarette. It looked huge in my small hand, and I cleared the empty wine bottles from the floor and shut off the TV before going back upstairs with a banana and an apple from the kitchen. I thought about letting the cigarette burn and eventually take the house down with it, as the fire would spread, but that would mean that the world would never see what I could become, and I couldn't have that. You may think I hated her for this, but that was never the case.

The next morning, I woke up with the sun on my face. I had never been a fan of sunshine. I preferred rain. I loved how everything went gray as if the sky itself was crying. It meant I was the only light in the world, and people needed me to survive. They needed to know their place.

I was home-schooled most of the time, whenever I wasn't practicing ballet, which was almost never, and as the years went on, Mother dropped my education altogether so I could solely focus on dancing.

I hadn't always lived in London. I grew up in New York and lived there till I was 10 years old. A year before we moved, Mother took me to see the ballet Swan Lake. It was the first time I had ever gone to the ballet, and I didn't understand why Mother insisted I go. I always knew I was brilliant, and I didn't need to see anyone else dance to know this. However, reluctantly, I agreed to go. Mother told me that it was important for me to see what I could achieve if I worked harder than anyone else, and for once in her miserable life, she was right. The enchantment I was left with afterward was unlike anything I had ever experienced anything I would ever experience again. I knew then that I wanted to utterly and completely immerse myself in the art of ballet, and I would give anything to dance as the Swan Princess and enchant the audience, who would become mesmerized as I poured my heart, blood, and soul out on stage, just for them. When Mother informed me that she had gotten a job in London at the Royal Ballet, I felt as if my whole world had come crumbling down. I was dragged to London, kicking and screaming the whole way. After refusing to acknowledge our new life even after we arrived in London, Mother managed to make me see reason. She made me realize that even though I wouldn't build my career in New York, London was one of the best, if not *the* best, places to work toward my dream.

She taught me the importance of turning any situation to my own advantage.

Chapter 2

I had been dancing in Mother's class at the Royal Ballet for 2 years. She was completely right about how the level of the dancers was higher here, but of course, no one was better than me. For the past year, I have been talking to Toby. One of the male dancers, whom I never particularly came to care for. But because of social norms, I had been made aware by Mother that I needed to talk to someone. Anyone. A man would never have been my first choice, as men generally are inferior to women; however, I had no idea how to talk to any of the girls in my class. They all just wanted to talk about braiding each other's hair at sleepovers and who was the cutest guy in school. None of that interested or concerned me, and it showed that they would never reach my level of dancing as they clearly didn't take it as seriously as the art of ballet demanded. So, I stuck with Toby. I never warmed to him, but he was drawn to me, and I mean, who can blame him?

For many years, it was just me and Toby, and I would use him to figure out how to act in social situations in exchange for giving him permission to hang out with me. It was always dull, but I kept reminding myself that I might need him later in life. For what, I didn't know yet, but if I ever needed something from him, we needed to be on good terms.

Now, there I stood, 19 years old, and the embarrassing excuse for a sign-up sheet was staring back at me. The words: AUDITIONS FOR SWAN LAKE were written in all caps with a dull pencil. The world stopped spinning as I picked up the pen. The chain that connected the pen to the board was roughly drilled into the board, and it was clear that whoever had been in charge of attaching it hadn't cared about how it would look when people came to sign their names. No one should care so little for their job.

Even the smallest and seemingly insignificant mistakes can lead to your life falling apart, and you would be left with no other option than simply observing as one disaster follows the other. The chain consisted of tiny, silver metal balls that glistened in the light from the afternoon sun. It was as if the pen needed protection in case someone had planned an intricate coup for the sole purpose of stealing it. How pathetic.

As I wrote my name at the bottom of the list filled with the names of people who were ignorant enough to believe that they deserved this more than me, everything went quiet. My dream of dancing as the Swan Princess at the Royal Ballet, which I had worked toward for 10 years of my life, was finally within reach. I could almost touch it.

I was never particularly fond of my name. CATHERINE LANGLEY. It stood out. It made me think of all the times Mother decided to pick me out of the ballet class and make an example of me. To use me as an example of what not to do, what not to look like, and what not to be like. You may think I despised her for that, but I never did. I believe it was one of the main reasons why I had come as far as I had. Our relationship was built on a solid foundation of professionalism. She was the only person I had ever met who understood the importance of taking the art of ballet seriously. As a child, I didn't understand why she would pick me apart in front of the other children. However, before I turned eight, I finally understood her motivations and came to love her for how she treated me. I stood out to her because she saw how perfect I could become if I were pushed far enough.

When I was seven, I decided to confront her and ask her why she kept singling me out in front of the other children. She sat in the brown leather chair with her feet up like she always did after a long day of teaching.

"Mama, can I ask you something?" I mumbled, too low for her to hear me.

"What? Don't mumble," she snapped back in a raspy voice.

She didn't move, and her eyes were closed as she spoke. Her head was resting on the back of the chair. She had always been an elegant woman, but her throat, collarbones, and chin were among the most beautiful sights I ever came across. It was exposed and vulnerable as she sat in her chair, and I was immediately taken back to the first time I thought about taking her life. It would have been beautiful.

"It makes me sad when you tell everyone I made a mistake," I answered in as confident a voice as I could find while plastering my eyes to the floorboards. I knew she hated it when I complained. I could feel the atmosphere change, and the tension was rising as I spoke.

"I am only doing what is best for you," she said, now looking directly at me with a stern look on her face as she exhaled a cloud of smoke.

"I have to make sure that you never make the same mistake twice. Eventually, you'll be perfect, but I have to be hard on you, do you understand?"

I didn't. It seemed unfair that she couldn't just be a happy mom, hug me, and take me out for ice cream after class like all the other moms.

"Do you?" she asked again, breaking me out of the trance I had accidentally gotten myself into.

"Yes, mama," I answered.

"Can we go out for ice cream? I did very well today, don't you think?" I asked while doing a twirl in my ballet clothes I hadn't changed out of yet.

"Not as well as you could have done." She said while shaking her head, and a smile of disbelief framed her face. She bent forward to reach the ashtray and put out her cigarette.

"Do you want me to help you, or do you want to be a nobody? Do you want to be like Aunt Tessa?" she asked. She had gotten up and began walking toward me. She always brought up Aunt Tessa when she wanted me to understand the importance of listening to her. She mentioned her to paint a picture of the life that I would be heading toward if I didn't do as I was told.

To paint you an image of Tessa, she had always been inferior to Mother in regard to beauty and skills in general. She had paranoid Schizophrenia, which made her hard to be around as she believed their dad was after her and wanted to kill her. I wouldn't be surprised if it were true, but since it is all she can talk about, it gets tiring after a while, and there are other things I would rather do with my precious time.

Because of this, I never visit her much. She is a danger to others, so she is at a facility with professionals somewhere. I never bothered to learn the details.

Mother stopped when she was just a few inches away from me. I felt her staring at me, searching for my eyes, but only found the back of my head. I felt like the smallest creature ever to exist. I failed to answer, as my own fear of what would come next had made my tongue double in size and my mouth dry like sandpaper.

"Answer me!" she roared, and as I had predicted, just as it had happened so many other nights before. I felt the cold, bony, skinny hand smack me across the face. The hand that had been so gentle in class, adjusting the other ballerinas to the correct positions, was now rough and merciless. Yet, it was not unfamiliar. I was the only one who ever got to experience the anger and harshness of her hands. I felt the tears silently streaming down my face as the red mark from her hand burned into my cheek.

"I don't, mama," I said as I tried to compose myself. "I will be perfect. I promise," I continued, under my breath, in between sobs.

Mother kneeled down, so we were now eye to eye. With the well-known cold and distant look in her eyes, she broke the silence.

"You will be the perfect ballerina, okay? I will make it so."

"Okay," I mumbled as I wiped my runny nose and wet eyes with the palm of my hand. My ballet clothes, which I usually associated with calmness and confidence, suddenly felt suffocating, and I needed to be released from them before they would force out every last breath I had within me.

"Go change your clothes and wash your hands. I'll make dinner in a minute."

I simply nodded and dragged my feet up the stairs. I cried silently, the way I had learned through the years so Mother wouldn't think I was weak.

Mother's words stayed with me throughout my entire life and made me realize that my name stood out on the sign-up sheet because I had worked harder than anyone else, and I wanted it more than anyone else.

What an ignorant and foolish child I was to think that ice cream was the way to my dreams. I treasure Mother's lessons as they were the main reason I managed to reach perfection.

I nodded my head in satisfaction as I took a step back and admired my name on the list. I had moved out of Mother's house three years earlier, and I looked forward to getting the letter in the mail that would tell me when and where the audition would take place without having Mother breathing into my neck, clinging on to how she used to make every decision for me. My victories used to be her victories. I did not need her anymore, but she failed to see that.

I knew that the role was mine. You may think that it was premature of me to believe so, but if you want something, you have to believe it. I believed it, and I wanted it.

As I was walking home, it started to rain. I have always loved the rain. It was as if the sky had opened just for me, and every drop was a tear. I danced through the rain as I made my way home and completely ignored the group of girls who waved and yelled at me from across the street. I had become absorbed in the city as the rain poured down upon it. It made every surface dance and come alive as the raindrops and the city became one entity.

I knew the girls from ballet class since we moved to London, but I never bothered to learn their names. One of them, the one I think was the leader of their group, always called me Cat. I hated that. Really, I hated anyone who called me anything other than Catherine. I had never seen the appeal of using pet names. They always end up being worse than the original name. And there must have been a reason your parents gave you your name in the first place, right? So why change it? It made no sense to me, but they could do whatever they wanted; they were of no use to me. I always saw them together, shopping, eating, drinking, going to parties, or something else. Everything they did was meaningless. Even as they danced in rehearsals, they spent too much time talking and giggling instead of focusing on what was really important. Dancing. I refused to socialize with people like them who hadn't managed to see the true purpose of life and wasted it away. Those kinds of people weren't welcome in my world if I had anything to say about it.

When I reached my door, I could hear Baryshnikov meowing from the other side of the door. I had been at the studio much longer than I promised when I left that morning, and I knew he would be hungry. As I stepped inside my apartment, a pool of water began to take form beneath me. I was more soaked than I realized.

"Damn it," I whispered to myself.

Baryshnikov meowed between slurps of rainwater. He seemed to enjoy it more than the water from the kitchen. A smile formed on my face as I was sure he could taste that it was a pool of tears from the sky. He was intelligent, which was part of why I loved him. I wasn't interested in surrounding myself with people or animals who were imbeciles.

As I took off my coat and boots and made sure it had been hung in a place where it wouldn't damage the hardwood floors, I fed Baryshnikov next. I appreciated him for many reasons, but the main reason I had kept him when I found him in the alley down the street two years prior was that he was the only male creature I had ever interacted with that was worth paying attention to and care for. Males have always been, and always will be, the inferior gender.

Chapter 3

The weeks went by faster than expected. I checked my e-mail every day, but not until Tuesday morning, three weeks after I signed up, did it arrive.

Auditions for The Swan Lake Ballet

Dear Ms. Langley

Thank you for your interest in our auditions for The Swan Lake Ballet. The auditions will be held on February 3rd and February 4th on the mainstage from 9 am till 5 pm. Please state your full name and age as well as the role(s) you wish to audition for, down below.

When we have received your registration, your audition schedule will be sent to you.

Thank you once again for your interest in participating in our production of the Swan Lake Ballet.

It took them long enough. I filled everything out as they asked and almost immediately received a response. February 3rd, 2 pm. It was only ten days away. Luckily, this is what I had been preparing for.

On the morning of my audition, I got up an hour before I usually would. I wanted to get a head start on rehearsing and perhaps put a face to the names from the sign-up sheet that were ignorant enough to think they stood a chance. Baryshnikov was wobbling sleepily down the hallway, attempting to follow me, but gave up halfway. He curled himself into a ball and fell back asleep against the wall so as not to be in my way.

I was out of the house thirty minutes after my alarm rang. Discipline is of utter importance, and perfection is sprouting from it.

It was a cold morning, and the city was not yet awake. As I turned the corner and found the building in my eyesight, I took a pause and allowed myself to enjoy how the darkness of the early morning wrapped around me. At the end of this day, my whole life would change.

As usual, I was the first person in the studio. I preferred it this way so I could put down my bag and inhibit the best corner of the room. I put down my bag with everything I might need during the day. I put in my headphones and floated away into my favorite universe. I felt myself dancing under the stars, my body completely surrendering to me and obeying every command. I looked in the mirror and made sure everything was perfect. Suddenly, I saw Mother in the reflection, walking around me, fixing me, and making sure I did not make any mistakes that she had seen before. I saw her hands in the mirror as they adjusted my leg mid-air. The second her hands touched my leg, a familiar rush ran through me, and as I locked eyes with her, a voice snapped me back to reality.

"Looks good," it was Toby, staring at me from the doorway.

"I know, Toby," I answered without looking away from the mirror.

I had known Toby for almost 10 years, but I never particularly liked him. To be fair, I never warmed to anyone. He was tall, lean, and very muscular. He had the ideal body for what he did, and I enjoyed dancing with him because he understood that his job was to put me on display and show the audience that I was the main attraction. Not everyone seemed to understand that, but Toby had never disappointed me in that regard.

I always knew that it was a waste of time to make friends, but it seemed that I was the only one who understood this. Toby never followed my way of thinking in that regard, and he acted as if we were friends. We hung out sometimes, sure, but I never said we were friends. I do not have any interest in making friends, and every time I said this to him, he laughed as if he thought it was a joke. I was not trying to be funny. That is just one example of why I didn't socialize with anyone.

"What are you rehearsing?" he asked.

"My audition," I snapped back at him in an attempt to make him understand that I was in no mood for conversation.

"Right, I saw your name on the sign-up sheet." He said, without realizing that I wanted him out.

It was a pointless statement that did not require a response. I saw his reflection in the mirror as he stepped further into the room, and I felt the frustration rise in me as I realized that he needed to interact with me before I could make him go away. He had not changed at all in the last three years except for his hair, which he had kept shorter to make sure he could control his curls. I removed my leg from the bar and began moving toward my bag while Toby slowly made his way across the room to me. I could hear his sloppy and heavy steps as his feet hit the floor. I visualized how his hair would bounce up and down ever so slightly with each step.

I always kept my hair in a tight bun, finished off with enough hairspray to freeze a flock of moving birds. I had to make sure that everything was flawless: my hair, my clothes, my breath, my posture, and my dance. I sat down to stretch on the floor, and without saying a word, Toby sat down next to me. He could have at least waited for an invitation. He talked, and I didn't respond. I was focused on being in the best shape for my audition, and I wanted to run through my routine at least once before 1.30 pm.

Finally, Toby stopped his waterfall of words for a second to breathe. I used this opportunity to get him out.

"Listen, I have to rehearse, and you need to get out. I'll talk to you later." I said as I ushered him out, gesturing toward the door. I had no intention of talking to him later.

He did not look surprised or stunned. He just smiled at the floor and bopped his head before he finally left me alone. He waved at me as he stood in the door. Moron.

-----

2 pm came around. I was dressed in all white to encompass the role as best I could. As I stood at the side of the stage and waited for them to call my name, I disappeared into the silence that had spread throughout the hall after the person before me had made it through their audition. It was comforting. I had practiced all day, and I was ready.

"Catherine Langley," the female voice rang calmly over the speakers. The sound of my name filled the room and broke the glass bubble made up from the silence. I confidently walked on stage with my head held high and bowed to the four people sitting 5 rows away from the stage.

"Whenever you're ready," the lady said and smiled. I did not smile back. I signaled to the sound guy that I was ready for the music to start. As the first notes began to play, I admired how my body knew exactly what to do, even before I gave the command. I loved how it felt when my arms and legs were in the air and how all eyes were on me. I was perfection. My moment was interrupted by the same lady who had called me onto the stage 5 minutes earlier.

"Thank you, Ms. Langley. We'll let you know," she said with the fake smile still plastered on her face.

I hadn't gotten the opportunity to finish my routine. The disrespect was unbelievable. Then again, I was certain that they knew early on that I was going to be their Swan Princess.

"Thank you," I answered, with a small bop of my head before I disappeared off the stage behind the black curtains that hung from the ceiling.

I walked back to the studio to stretch and change out of my audition clothes. My mind was racing with all kinds of possible outcomes of my audition. Yet, they all ended with me dancing as the Swan Princess, night after night.

As I turned the corner and entered the room, I was met with the sight of Toby practicing basic ballet poses and movements. I did not stop to observe him, but I did find three flaws in his Rond De Jambe A Terre. I didn't bother to correct him. If he didn't know how to do this by now, he would never learn. Inevitably, Toby approached me and asked about my audition. He did not correct his mistakes before he decided he was done. This was a prime example of why men are impossible to be around. If he did not take the time to correct himself, how would he ever improve?

"It was fine," I answered him without making eye contact, packing up my stuff as fast as I could without seeming impolite. I was sure Baryshnikov would be hungry by now.

"Knowing you, I am sure it was more than fine." Toby countered with a gentle laugh; I knew, of course, that he was right. He may have been an idiot who couldn't read a room for the life of him, but he was the only person I ever talked to who understood how perfect I would be as the Swan Princess.

"I know," I answered, making sure there was no change to detect in my facial expression. I flung my bag on my shoulder and began walking toward the door. I was uncomfortably aware of Toby and how he kept talking to me, and I knew I cut him off by leaving the room. I didn't care. I needed to change and go back home.

It hadn't occurred to me how tired I was until I opened the door to my apartment, and the sweet smell of herbal tea flew into my face. Baryshnikov didn't bother to get up from the sofa when I entered, and I didn't seek him out either. This is just one example of why we work as housemates. I made his dinner, not caring if he ate it or not. I went through the hall, past the living room, and into my bedroom with the door closed. I quickly went to bed and fell into a dreamless sleep. I couldn't wait to hear back about the audition.

Chapter 4

10 days went by without a word, and I began to grow impatient. Another two days went by before the roles were announced. I confidently went online and found the list of the roles with the names of the people who had been cast next to it. My body began to shake with disappointment when I saw The Swan Princess at the top of the sheet, next to the name, OPHELIA COLLEY. I had never heard of her before. I immediately googled her name. She was 18 years old and had only been in two other productions. None of them had been at this level. She was completely unqualified and way too inexperienced to dance my role.

I had to get out of the house. Baryshnikov had made the smart and safe decision to stay out of my way until the frustrations let go of me. I went to the only place that stood a chance of calming me down. I saw several missed calls from Mother that I ignored. I needed to dance. I needed to practice the art that I knew nobody would be able to embody better than me. I needed to bear witness to the perfection that arose in the mirror as my body responded to my commands effortlessly.

I couldn't complain. That was the number one rule in the house growing up. Mother had never tolerated people who complained, and I refused to be upset about the letdown of not getting the role. As I turned the corner, my neck began to twitch as I realized that the roles had been posted on the board in the hall, as well as online, and everyone would know that I wouldn't be the one to dance as the Swan Princess. I held my head high and walked into the building, focused on my route to the rehearsal studio I knew would be empty. I walked fast, silently, and steadily so as not to attract attention and be drawn into the cluster of women clawing their way through the group to see if their name was on the list.

My headphones were at full volume, yet I was completely aware of everything going on around me. It is incredible how much you can tell from a person's character just by observing them for 5 seconds. I saw how people broke down when their names were nowhere to be seen. I saw people screeching as they saw they had gotten the role they wanted. I stopped for a second to see if I could spot Ophelia. I needed to know what she looked like, how she moved, and what made her better than me.

A girl I had danced with since we were kids came up to me with a giant smile on her face. I loved seeing women smile. It was so elegant and simple. Something so pure, just waiting to be ruined.

She interrupted my search for Ophelia and talked to me as if we were best friends. I wasn't in the mood to talk, but it is important to be polite, and I tried to keep up with her excitement and the subject of the conversation even though I continuously felt like I was ten seconds behind her.

"Have you seen it, have you seen it?" she asked, in a voice that was too high pitched.

"Yeah, I am really happy for her," I answered hesitantly.

"She is suuuch a great dancer! Have you ever seen her perform? I have. My mom and dad took me to see the Nutcracker that she was in. It was marvelous!" she took a breath while spinning around in excitement, only to face me again and continue talking. How could one person have so many words inside them all at once?

"And now you and I and all the others get to dance alongside her! Isn't that just exciting? I can't wait! Are you ready for tomorrow?" she eventually asked.

I realized then that I hadn't checked if I had gotten another role.

"What do you mean tomorrow?" I asked, with the hope that this girl could provide me with some answers.

"Oh, silly," she said as she touched my arm and lowered the pitch in her voice ever so slightly while looking away for a moment before our eyes met again. I never liked to be touched and quickly jerked my arm away and took a step back to make sure I was out of reach.

"We are both a part of the ensemble." She answered with an ecstatic smile and her regular, uncomfortable, high-pitched voice.

I rushed through the crowd of people that had multiplied in the time I had spent talking to the girl. I had to see if what she said was true. As I stood in front of the paper that replaced the sign-up sheet I had stared back at only a few weeks ago, I saw my own name next to Swan number 3. How humiliating. I had been made into a wallflower that no one would remember when they drove home to their miserable lives after living in a fantasy at the ballet. My eyes widened, and I felt more people joining the group. I continued toward the empty rehearsal studio and pretended I didn't hear the girl yell at me from a distance. "See you tomorrow!" she basically screamed as I tried to take my mind far away from reality.

When I returned home, I hung up my jacket and put my boots in their right place before going to the kitchen to find food for Baryshnikov.

"Shut up." I snapped as he kept meowing at me.

I sat down with a cup of tea and looked at the e-mail with the list of who had been cast in which roles. Toby had gotten the role of Benno. I knew he wouldn't shut up about it tomorrow. I quickly skipped over Ophelia's name and saw another unknown name next to Prince Siegfried. MAXIMILLAN REYNARD. It was another name I didn't know, but it didn't bother me. I would see him at rehearsal tomorrow, and if his technique was precise enough not to ruin the production altogether, I really could not care less about him.

I was the second person to arrive at the rehearsal. As I entered the room and looked around, I only saw a girl I hadn't seen before standing in the corner, speaking loudly into her cell phone. I ignored her while I made my way to the far corner on the opposite side of the room to put down my bag and begin my warmup. As the minutes ticked by, the room filled with the rest of the company, who slowly inhibited their chosen space on the floor. It seemed like everyone knew somebody, and once again, I was grateful that I hadn't wasted my time making friends in the past. I was in my own world as Toby inevitably approached me.

"Hey, how are ya? You excited?" he asked, with a goofy smile on his face. I couldn't help but find it strengthening my belief that males were never meant to socialize with anyone when

21

he abbreviated his words and changed it. There was no point in doing so.

"Hey, Toby. Yeah, it's great," I answered with as much enthusiasm as I could muster while facing away from him, focusing on the movement of my right foot.

I felt the excitement within him rise as the conversation progressed into the subject of him and the role he had gotten.

"Did you see the role I got?" he asked.

"Yeah, congratulations. I'm sure you will be fine." I answered and tried to sound as convincing as possible. It wasn't that Toby was a bad dancer, but he was nowhere near the best, either. He was extremely mediocre, and I wasn't sure he would be able to capture the audience. It really wasn't his fault, and it's not like he chose to be born as a male, where perfection was further out of reach than it would ever be for females.

"Yeah, thanks. I'm excited," he said as he no longer was able to contain his excitement and began to smile uncontrollably as he leaned on the bar and looked out over the room.

The door opened once again, and someone I had never laid eyes on before walked in. She floated across the floor, and everything began to move in slow motion. She wore a beautiful loose skirt over her tights and a tight-fitting black top to go with it. She was a beautiful creature. She briefly looked at me, and our eyes met. An unfamiliar feeling arose in me. It was a mixture of frustration and admiration, and her deep brown eyes had me mesmerized. Her ponytail swung left to right as she walked, and when she turned her head, a small strand of her long, brown, curly hair fell across her eyes and forehead. Her neck was lean, and her muscles and tendons were shifting between being visible and invisible as she moved her head around the room to scan the company for people she knew. Her collarbones were perfectly symmetrical, and I was fascinated by how her head and throat were connected to the rest of her body. I imagined what she would look like without a throat — her vocal cords and tendons destroyed and removed from her elegant body. I wondered how she would look with her head placed onto her torso, without a throat to connect the pieces.

I was brought back to reality as Toby put his hand on my shoulder, and the woman began moving at a normal pace as the rest of the world came back to me. She continued, unharmed, and floated toward some guy she apparently knew. Her eyes lit up, along with a smile on her face as they saw each other.

"Max!" I heard her screech as she threw her arms around his neck. Deeply unprofessional.

"Ophelia!" I heard him say in a lower voice with the same excitement as he wrapped his arms around her petite torso.

I knew that Toby had been talking to me, but I didn't have any interest in finding out what he had said.

"Well, I'll go warm up." Toby finally said. I hoped he hadn't noticed that I hadn't been paying attention.

"Yeah, great. I'll see you." I breathed. She was not what I had expected.

The artistic director addressed us collectively before we were to split up and rehearse our particular choreography. We had all been doing movements by the bars while she had been observing us. I found my eyes constantly drifting toward Ophelia. I felt myself drawn to her, and the need to find out what kind of creature she was filled my mind. I knew these movements like the back of my hand and adored how my body did them perfectly, automatically. I was hyper-aware of the sound of the ballet shoes clicking as they hit the floor, all at the same time. I let the rhythm surround me, and the calming feeling filled my mind. None of us knew what the director was looking for. I was focused on Ophelia and how the muscles in her back were working as her body moved.

"Thank you," the director's voice pierced through the rhythm and made it stop instantly.

"You, you, you, and you," she said as she pointed to four girls I didn't know. "Stay behind. The rest of you split up to the different rooms assigned to your roles."

A low muttering of voices encapsulated the room as the dancers began to scatter. Toby stopped me on my way toward the door.

"I will never get tired of watching you dance," he said. "I don't know how you do it every time." he continued as he shifted his eyes from me to the floor. He dragged his foot right to left on the floor between us.

I couldn't help feeling proud.

"Thanks, Toby. You're not so bad yourself." I answered with a hesitant smile.

"Do you know what the four girls are doing in here? What was that about?" I asked. I knew that Toby was more involved in the social aspect of the ballet, and if I gave him a small smile and a bit of eye contact, I could make him tell me everything I needed to know.

His face lit up as I asked my question. I never let him help me, so he treasured it when he was rarely allowed.

"Yeah," He stood up a little straighter than before and puffed out his chest a bit while trying to sound as nonchalant as he could.

"They'll be the four dancers for the Dance of The Little Swans in the second act." He continued. My smile faded instantly. Once again, they had failed to see my potential.

"Okay, great," I said harshly, avoiding Toby's attempt to make eye contact.

"Sooo, I was wond-" He began, before I cut him off by turning around and continuing my walk to the door. As I walked, I thought about Ophelia. How could she possibly deserve this more than me?

Chapter 5

I got up one and a half hours earlier than I usually would. I noticed that my shoes were close to falling apart at the end of rehearsals the day before, and I wouldn't tolerate my shoes sabotaging my perfection. I decided to bring an extra pair, and I needed to break them in before I left for the studio.

I have always loved the process of breaking in my ballet shoes. When you first take them out of the box, they look fragile and innocent. They are hard and soft at the same time, and my favorite part of this beautiful process is cracking the soles of the shoes and scraping the bottom. It is a brilliant activity, and I get absorbed into it. I become mesmerized by ruining something so precisely created just for me to break. The power it gave me was exhilarating.

I put them on and moved around in my living room. I had a slim full-sized mirror on the wall, next to my sofa. I admired my technique and noticed how I had perfected the art of breaking in my shoes over the years.

As I walked to the studio, I had Tchaikovsky's music blasting into my head. I noticed Toby behind me on his old, rugged bike. Had he seriously taken a longer route to the studio just so that he would go past my apartment? I will never understand the simple and underdeveloped minds of men.

"Hey!" He said, out of breath, as he swung the leg of his bike and began dragging it alongside him. He increased his pace to catch up to me, his bag flapping on his back.

"Hey," I said. "Do you usually take this route?" I asked, wanting him to tell me all his deepest, darkest secrets.

"No, not exactly." he stammered as if he was surprised by my question.

"All right," I said in a monotone voice.

I liked that Toby never expected me to contribute very much to our conversations. I could take from it what I found useful and throw away the rest.

"Have you seen that new girl, Ophelia? She's really good," he said, and immediately caught my attention. I kept calm and intended to utilize our time walking to find out what he knew.

"Yeah, she looks great," I said, hoping it was enough for Toby to open up.

"Great? More like brilliant!" he said, and it became harder for me to hide my anger and frustrations.

Toby had been around Maximillian and Ophelia in rehearsal, and his descriptions of their performances seemed too good to be true.

"You should come by this afternoon," he said suddenly, "we usually work till 9 pm. But it would be great to see you later, and we could walk home together afterward," he continued, and I noticed his cheeks turning red. It was getting pathetic.

I went over my options in my head. This was my way in to observe her and be in the same room as she would be dancing in, and hopefully (but probably not), she would mesmerize me with her dancing. I would be able to make my own assessment of whether or not she was enchanting and technically good enough for the role that was rightfully mine. Would she bring the same to the role that I would have? I strongly doubted it.

"Sure," I said. "I'll come by and watch when we're done."

"Great!" Toby said way too loudly while his face lit up. I almost hadn't finished my sentence before he blurted out his answer.

My body was more tired than usual after thc rehearsals that day. The only reason I didn't break my promise to Toby was the opportunity to observe Ophelia.

I hurried out of the room, so no one had the chance to capture me and force me into a conversation I had no interest in participating. As I entered the room, I was met with the sight of Maximillian and Ophelia rehearsing their pas de deux from the second act. The spectators in the room were still and quiet. I closed the door silently so as not to interrupt. I silently made my way to a chair in the corner of the room. I saw Toby being focused even though he wasn't dancing. Everyone was watching their duet, and now, so was I. I saw Ophelia completely surrendering to Maximillian. She trusted him not to let her fall, and I will admit that they were good. However, not as good as I would have been. I became unconsciously focused on how Maximillian's hands ran across Ophelia's back, how his hands connected to hers, the look in his eyes, the look in her eyes. The pounding in my chest increased until the end. Everyone in the room seemed to have held their breath, and when they finished, everyone let a sigh leave their body. I saw the potential in them, but it was a bit of an overreaction. It was beautiful, sure, but far from perfect. They were relying too much on their emotions to carry them through, and that was simply unacceptable. Small mistakes, which I stopped making at the age of eight, were something they still weren't able to get right. I couldn't believe this was the best they could come up with.

I didn't move a muscle throughout their rehearsal. I didn't acknowledge Toby as he attempted to give me a subtle smile and catch my eye. He was ridiculous.

The dancers all looked happy. A meaningless emotion that wouldn't lead to anything useful, but it seemed as if people around you and the society appreciated and trusted you more if you were smiling and simulating happiness. I had become very good at faking this with years of practice.

Around 8 pm, Toby and the close ensemble were free to go. I hadn't noticed the time since I got there. I ignored Toby as he began to move towards me.

"Hey, glad you could make it." He said with a stupid smile. "Aren't they just terrific?" He asked, slightly out of breath, with a hand on each hip peering in the direction of Maximillian and Ophelia. He seemed to be in deep wonder about what he had just witnessed. The fact that he couldn't see that would be the overstatement of the year. I had to fight the urge to roll my eyes at him until they got stuck in the back of my head, and I would lose my sight forever. Males were never aware of the small and most important things. I decided to hide my disgust for his statement and gave him a small smile. She had been dancing beautifully.

"Sure, beautiful," I said, while my eyes followed Ophelia as she walked across the room chatting with people she barely knew. I noticed her throat as she threw her head back in laughter. Perhaps Toby noticed I looked at her instead of paying attention to our conversation. He eventually interrupted me.

"She's really sweet, too." He said and paused while staring at the side of my head. "Mm-hmm," I breathed in response. "Do you want me to introduce you?" he asked me while I continued to stare at her, noticing her movements and body.

My heart skipped a beat. I didn't expect him to introduce us, but without hesitation, I agreed. I hadn't had time to think it through. How does one go about meeting new people? No one new had become a part of my life since I was a child. I nodded my head and hoped that Toby would take the lead, and all I would have to do would be to smile politely.

We walked up to her while she and Maximillian were discussing something I didn't hear. It was probably not something that was worth wasting time on, anyway. I made sure that my breath was good and my hands weren't sweaty. Toby walked in front of me, and when we were just a few inches away from her, he gently tapped her shoulder. She turned around, and her luscious, curly hair swung around in the air, landing on her shoulder. Suddenly, I was faced with her dark eyes, and a smile formed on her lips when she saw Toby's face. Would she ever light up like that at the sight of me?

"Toby!" She exclaimed as she put her hand on his arm. "Who's your friend?" she asked, looking at me.

"This is Catherine, Catherine, this is Ophelia," Toby stated while pointing his hand to the person whose name was being said. He took a step back.

"Nice to meet you." She said in a smooth and graceful voice, shaking my hand and looking into my eyes. I took note of every bone I felt in her hand how they would be exposed to the sun if her skin had been peeled back. Her nails were natural and a little longer than I would have chosen. Yet, the length would make it easy to tear them from her fingertips, and the blood would dance around us—her screams like music. Like the rest of her body, her hands were slender, elegant, and soft. She would never expect it. I thought about what it would feel like to hold her the way Maximillian did. How it would feel to be someone she surrendered to and trusted completely. I wanted to run my hands across every inch of her skin until nothing was left untouched. The spots that Maximillian had touched, I would have to touch twice.

No one had ever looked at me like that before. It was as if she was genuinely interested in who I was. I didn't know the proper way to react, so I simply smiled back at her and shook her hand. I refused to give her access to anything.

"You too," I mumbled, lower than intended.

"So, what did you think?" she asked while gesturing into the room that had emptied as people had left to take a break.

"It was great," I said enthusiastically. "The way you managed to convey the feelings at play is beautiful".

She looked happy and satisfied with my response. It wasn't entirely wrong or a lie. It was great, not fantastic. It was beautiful, not enchanting. It didn't seem to bother her, and I was glad I wasn't required to explain myself further.

Chapter 6

I tossed and turned for hours that night. Ophelia refused to leave my mind, and eventually, I gave up on sleep. Baryshnikov was clearly confused about why I suddenly moved around at 2 am, yet he dealt with it and followed me into the kitchen, where I made a cup of herbal tea. I ignored him and accepted that he was following me around, even though I would rather have been alone. I went into my living room and sat down in my pajamas and fluffy white slippers that were a size too big.

I thought about Mother. I thought about how she showed up in the reflection in the mirror when I was working on my audition piece. It was as if she knew that I would be unsuccessful, and she was warning me that I should not even think about complaining when I would inevitably fail. Her piercing eyes were haunting me. Ophelia and our interaction once again got a hold on my mind and did not let go. Instead of fighting it and pushing her away, I surrendered and gave in.

I sat down in my purple armchair, which was placed directly across from the mirror, and allowed the light of night to surround and encapsulate me. I saw my own reflection staring back at me. Everything had suddenly gone quiet, and as the seconds moved slower than they ever had, Ophelia's silhouette began to form behind me in the mirror. I didn't move. I became focused on how her figure slowly began to show. I noticed how it looked as if her body extracted every color around her into itself. She became more and more colorful as the room around her turned grey and lifeless. At first, she simply stood behind me, and we watched ourselves and each other in the reflection. She was wearing a red flowy dress that moved, even though there was no wind anywhere nearby. She began to move toward me, and I found myself feeling anxious and excited at the same time. I wanted her to touch me. I wanted our bodies to be intertwined and for us to be entangled in each other. When she was only an inch away from me, she bent down and whispered my name into my ear. I closed my eyes as I felt her breath on my skin. Suddenly, everything felt completely right and suffocating at the same time. When she put her hand on my shoulder, I couldn't take it anymore. If I was not careful, I would surrender to her completely, and everything I had worked for would be ruined. I refused to let it happen. I saw myself grab her wrist and twist it until I heard her bones breaking. The next thing I remember is seeing myself sitting on top of her while searching for the pain and fear in her eyes. But it was not there; only a slight and frustrating smile formed on her face. I grabbed her throat between my hands and jammed her head into the hardwood floors of my living room repeatedly while screaming, "NO, NO, NO!" through gritted teeth. I continued until I heard and felt the back of her head crack open, and the pool of blood began to seep around her head, staining my hardwood floors. She stopped moving. The scene suddenly disappeared when I looked up and locked eyes with my reflection in the mirror. I was now staring back at myself, sitting in my purple armchair once again.

She had gained a power over me that I had not allowed, and therefore, she had to suffer. I needed to take control of her and her life and make sure that she knew she wasn't worth anything.

I found my little black book in the bottom drawer of my dresser. It had been hidden away for many years, and it had never been opened. I didn't remember where I had gotten it, but I didn't care. I hadn't known what to write in it, but now it had a purpose. I would dedicate this book to Ophelia. Everything there was to know about her would be written in this book and kept, just for me. My goal was to gain full control of her, make her suffer, and show not only myself but also Mother, Ophelia, and everyone who had a false image of me that nobody was better than me. People could try to control me, but I would never let them, and I would retaliate so harshly that they would never attempt it again.

I began with the basics and took out my computer. Social media was a great place to begin my project. I began by going on Facebook and writing her name in the search bar. She came up as the first person, and her dark curly hair shone and stood out on the screen. I pressed the profile, and at first, it did not look as if there was anything out of the ordinary, only the usual pictures of her and her friends partying, showing off their lives because their lives are basically empty if they don't share it with the world on the internet. Her profile picture is a close-up of her laughing goofily, her head thrown back, exposing her neck. I let my finger run across her neck on the screen, imagining what it would be like to touch it in real life.

I scrolled down her page, and she hadn't been posting very much. It was about two or three posts a year, which was obviously too much but better than what other people believed was necessary. I wrote down her birthday and all of the cities that she had been living in prior to living in London. I noticed that her cover photo was of herself and Maximillian dancing in rehearsal. Hatred, anger, and frustration rose within me as I looked closer and noticed how his hands held her. She was thrown back, and Maximillian was holding and supporting her. The look of lust in his eyes was especially infuriating as he clearly wasn't aware of his place. There was no way that he would ever be good enough to have her surrender to him. If they became a couple, I knew that it would be up to me to stop it and make them both realize how wrong it was for them.

But that was a concern for another time. First, I needed to build a foundation for Ophelia. I had to figure out who was dearest to her. If I gained that information, it might open a creative opportunity to hurt her. She hadn't posted any family members on Facebook, so I had to dive into that part of her life through different channels. I was stuck on her page for hours, scrolling through all her pictures and events. It was mostly pictures of her dancing and being out with her so-called friends. If they were really her friends, they would tell her that she didn't have what it takes, but I have come to realize that only I had the ability to tell people the truth.

I made a mental note to ask Toby about her the next day. People seemed to enjoy his company, and Ophelia seemed very friendly with him when I was introduced to her. I knew exactly how to act to get Toby to tell me what he knew. It was almost too easy. I closed my laptop and laid down the book on the table next to it. The book looked like a dark black hole that would drag all signs of life out of its surroundings. It made me feel at ease, and after I drank the last of my tea, I curled up in my chair and fell into a dreamless sleep.

The next morning, I went about my usual routine with a still wobbly and confused Baryshnikov following me around. Once again, he was a great example of how male creatures were unable to adapt to new situations and complained when things did not go according to their own head. I didn't bother paying too much attention to him, and when I turned around after locking my door, Toby was walking down the street in my direction. I plastered on a fake but believable smile and saw him pick up the pace to reach me.

"Hey!" he yelled way too excitedly. "Ready for the day?" I didn't know how he wanted me to respond to that. Of course, I was ready. What kind of question was that? I swallowed my disgust for him, widened my eyes, and smiled at him while nodding. None of us spoke for the first few minutes of our walk, and Toby almost crashed his bike into a tree on the side of the road because he was too mesmerized by me. I understand him, but he is stupid if he genuinely believes we would ever begin a romantic relationship. We laughed it off, and as I ran my hands through my hair, I decided to use this break of silence to begin my questioning of him.

"So…have you talked with Ophelia lately?" I paused when I noticed the surprise on his face. I guess he was too self-involved to understand why I was asking that question. Luckily, that played to my advantage as he then wouldn't figure out the real reason for my interest. This was my project, and I wanted no one to know about it until I had a finished product to present.

"A little. She's mostly occupied with rehearsal, though." Okay, so I had to work a bit for him to open up. I gladly accepted the challenge.

"Yeah, I can imagine," I sighed without returning his rigorous attempt at making eye contact. He could be rewarded when he gave me what I wanted.

"Do you know if she has been in anything we would have heard of before coming here?" That was obviously a trick question. I already knew that she hadn't done a lot. However, I didn't know why. There must have been a reason. Of course, I had to give myself a break, as I had only had a few hours of research time the night before. I would have plenty of time in the following days. I was only just getting started.

"Yeah, I mean, she has done mostly local stuff, or "originals" …" Toby put both hands next to his head, making air quotes, almost causing his bike to fall to the ground. He paused for a second and took a sharp breath of panic while grabbing his falling bike. "They weren't especially successful. But apparently, someone from the theater went to one of her performances by chance and asked her to audition for our production."

That's it, Toby. Give me more.

"There are rumors about her and Max, but I don't know if it's reliable," Toby said this as if it didn't mean anything. It meant a great deal. There was no way that Maximillian and Ophelia could be together or have any kind of relationship that goes beyond friendship. She would never reach my level of perfection, but she was the only one in the production with the potential, and she shouldn't allow Maximillian to have her in that way. She was better than that.

Obviously, I couldn't let my true feelings about this show when Toby was near, so I shrugged in response and was grateful that we had made it to the theater. I kept up the successful facade until we went our separate ways to our rehearsal studios.

After rehearsal, I took my time packing my bag. That did result in unpleasant conversations with girls who were too shallow to interact with, but I knew that I had to endure this if I wanted to spend my evening the way I had planned. As the room came alive and people scattered, I took a minute to look at my phone. A notification from Facebook that I removed without looking at its contents, as well as two missed calls from Mother and a text from Toby asking me to "Hang out" after rehearsal, took up the screen. I knew that Mother was waiting to hear from me, but I honestly did not have the energy or the capacity to deal with her drunk calls. I ignored her, as usual, and blew off Toby. I had better and more important things to take care of tonight.

At last, I was the only person left in the room. It had gone quiet like a tomb. It was cold, suffocating, and comforting at the same time. I was in my element. I felt invincible as I stood in front of the mirror, staring at my reflection. I enjoyed observing how my body obeyed me, and the perfection and techniques that I was able to execute were breathtaking. It reminded me of what I was working for, and the end result would be mine, eventually. Ophelia may be a good dancer, but because of that, she was also my greatest threat, and I had to eliminate her before it got out of hand. I went to my corner of the room, pulled my bag over my shoulder, and headed for the door to find Ophelia. I only wanted to see where she went when she wasn't at rehearsal. When it comes down to it, none of us really knew her, but that would soon change. The plan was to wait for her to leave the theater and follow her wherever she went. I needed to know the roots of her being, and the best place to begin this part of my research was to discover where she lived.

I was stopped in my train of thought by a group of laughing and squeaking wannabe ballerinas who walked past the door. When I looked back into the mirror before I closed the door, I saw Mother at the back of the room. I didn't move. She shook her head while maintaining eye contact with me through the mirror, but she had done much worse in her time and had no right to judge me and my thoughts.

"Go to hell." I hissed before I closed the door, leaving my mother to suffocate in the silence.

Chapter 7

As the day ended, I kept a watchful eye on Ophelia. My plan commenced now, and I would continue to work on it until I physically couldn't keep my eyes open. I had hoped that she would walk straight home; however, that hope was gone as soon as I left the studio. We had made our way outside, and I had deliberately avoided Toby to make sure that I wasn't held up in a pointless conversation that took way more energy than I could afford. I heard Toby faintly calling my name from the entrance, but my focus was solely on Ophelia and the group of girls that followed her around. It was Friday, the end of the week, which I hadn't calculated into my plans. What if she went somewhere other than home? I had to try and follow her anyway, and so I did.

As I had expected, the group of girls and Ophelia went straight to the bar that was located a few blocks away from the studio. "God Dammit…" I muttered to myself, angry at my own miscalculations. Not only did I not know where she lived, but because of all the other girls, it would be too risky following them inside. Too many eyes. I decided to go home instead and follow her a few days later. Patience was key to my plan, and I intended to remain in control.

When I walked into my apartment, I remembered Baryshnikov for the first time that day. I fed him, as usual, and made my own herbal tea as I sat down in front of my computer. I hadn't bothered to change out of my clothes from rehearsals, as they made me feel empowered and in control of everything I did. It was my armor, and with it, I could do anything.

Because she hadn't been in many productions, it was harder than I expected to find something useful to put into my black book.

After searching on Google for a while, I decided to go back to her Facebook page and hope that she had listed family members. Luckily, her mother was easy to find. The familiarity was uncanny. The same straight teeth and long brown curls. However, their eyes were different, and her mother lacked the natural beauty that encapsulated Ophelia.

As I looked through the Facebook page of the mother, I found Ophelia's grandmother. I wrote down all the names of the family members I could find, but I underlined Mary Colley, as I expected that she was important to Ophelia based on the fact that the cover photo on Mary's page was of the two of them together. I smiled and took a sip of my tea. I was definitely on to something. I saw a birthday greeting from Ophelia that supported my suspicion. It was some sticky message with a bunch of hearts and love and other crap. Nothing of importance, but I could see that Ophelia loved her. If I got to the grandmother, I would get to Ophelia.

Before my investigation could continue, I noticed my phone almost vibrating itself off the table. It was late at night, and only Mother would call at this hour.

"Hello?" I answered in an irritated voice. I didn't have time for her right now, but she did make me who I was, so I guess I owed her a phone call after ghosting her for weeks.

"Hey Catherine," Mother's voice was drunken and cold.

"What's up?" I asked, already eager for the conversation to end.

"I juss wann tell you.."

"Mother, you trailed off. What?" I said while pushing the phone into the side of my head and scrunching my face to better focus on her words. She was drunk. I hated it when she was drunk.

"I cannot believe you didn't get it. What did you do?" She slurred.

"I don't know, Mother. I did everything you taught me and more. Look, I can't talk right now, but I'll call later in the week."

"But you gotta t-"

I hung up. I had too much on my mind to let myself be distracted by her. That was worries for another day.

I continued my research on the grandmother. Unlike Ophelia, Mary had been doing quite a lot. She used to dance when she was young, and the pictures were eminent. After she retired from dancing, she bought an old building and converted it into a dance studio for children. "pffh, children.." I muttered to myself with a smile of pity on my face. I could never imagine being around children that much. Even when I was a child myself, I thought they were annoying. Not only were they noisy and disgusting, but they had no sense of personal space, and I remember that I always wished that there would be one less child who showed up to every class. Sadly, they all showed up every time.

However, the grandmother looked like she enjoyed her work. There were pictures on the website so families could see what the place looked like before they signed up for their child. I looked through the pictures, scanning for Ophelia, and suddenly, the familiar mesmerizing brown curls and glistening smile caught my eye. Ophelia was standing in the newly renovated dance studio in front of what seemed like a thousand children. They all stood with their arms above their head and their legs on the beam. I could easily see that none of them had the potential to become memorable, and I pitied them in regard to how their parents told them they could be anything. That was the biggest lie any parent could ever tell a child.

In another picture, Ophelia stood with her right arm around Mary's shoulders, and the identical smiles stared back at me next to the text SIGN UP NOW! How pathetic and needy they seemed. But it was perfect for me. I wrote down the address of the studio and decided that on the weekend after next, when I had one day off from rehearsals, I would pay the grandmother and the studio a visit.

Chapter 8

I closed the book and looked at the clock above the dresser that read 3:22. I knew it was time for bed, but I felt a need to continue and stayed up 30 minutes longer, looking around the website. When I reluctantly closed my computer, I went to bed with a satisfying feeling, and I couldn't wait to find out exactly where Ophelia lived and finally get under her skin.

On Monday, I decided to follow Ophelia once again. I had remembered to dress warmer than normal, as I wasn't aware of how far I had to walk after rehearsal finished. I just needed to find a way to make sure Toby didn't come with me.

After my team finished for the day, I went into the studio where the close ensemble rehearsed in the hope that Ophelia would be there and, hopefully, I would get a look at her and perhaps catch a smell of her perfume. I walked in just as the Swan Princess was transformed into the Black Swan. Sure, she conveyed the feelings necessary, but she lacked poise and precision, and her technique could have been better. The frustration rose in me again. I couldn't believe that they chose her over me. Only a man could have made such a terrible decision. However, I loved seeing her body at work. All the muscles and tendons, especially in the neck and upper chest. They seemed like they were just waiting for me to rip her apart. But I had to be patient.

As I walked in, Toby was standing to the side and had a moment which he spent on waving at me. I acted as if I didn't see him. I was completely focused on Ophelia, and I attempted to catch the feelings that were beginning to form in my stomach. Was it frustration, hate, or admiration? Whatever it was, I tried to keep it at a low point. I couldn't risk bursting in front of everybody.

After they finished the dance, everyone applauded, and afterward, everyone was sent home for the evening except for Maximillian and Ophelia. My heart dropped, as I saw Toby walk rapidly toward me while my eyes were still fixed on Ophelia and the way her hair bounced around as she nodded in understanding to what the ballet Mistress told them.

"Hey! What a nice surprise!" Toby yelled way too loudly. I'm sure it was to make everyone aware that he knew me. Just pathetic.

"Hey, keep your voice down," I answered sharply through gritted teeth.

"Why? What's going on?" Toby whispered while moving closer to me. The smell of his cologne was so disgusting that I had to close my eyes to keep the vomit down. It was nauseating to think that he believed I honestly could be attracted to him, especially with that cologne. I put a hand to my throat, which only made him come closer.

"Oh god, are you okay? You don't look too good."

"Yeah, I'm fine. I think I just need some water," I answered as a way to get away from him.

"Yes, of course," He said worriedly. As he went to leap toward his bag and his water bottle, he held out his arms and lifted his eyebrows in a "Please keep standing until I come back"-motion. I slowly nodded. I needed him to go away. As I looked down, I noticed a phone. It was on top of a pink bag (of course, it was pink), which had a name tag on it. It read *Ophelia.* I gasped silently and tapped the phone screen lightly to gain a, however tiny, insight into what went on when she was on her phone. When I saw her lock screen, my heart dropped to the floor, and it felt like it went up in flames of rage. It was a picture of Maximillian kissing Ophelia's cheek.

Chapter 9

After I saw that picture, everything moved as if I was in a haze. I pushed Toby away from me and went for the door. Screw it, I would gain her trust another day. I was enraged at her but also at Maximillian. How could they! It was so unprofessional!

When a hand grabbed my shoulder, I snapped:

"Back off, Toby!"

"Hey, I just want to help you."

I froze. It was Ophelia. I felt every muscle, every bone, and every skin cell of her hand pressing into my sweater. It was wonderful and painful at the same time.

"I'm sorry, I thought you were-"

"Toby?" Ophelia interrupted with a shy, enchanting, and understanding smile.

"Yeah," I said with probably the most fake smile I have ever plastered on my face in my life.

"Can I walk you out?" Ophelia asked suddenly. It caught me quite off guard, and her facial expression showed concern when I looked confused.

"Sorry, yeah, of course," I said in as natural a tone as I could manage. I didn't want her to notice how excited I was. Maybe today would go to plan after all.

As we began to walk, I could smell her perfume, even through all the layers we were both wearing. She smelled like vanilla and strawberries. It was a stark contrast to the heavy stench of cigarettes and old wine that I was used to from our house back in New York.

"So, how are you feeling? I figured the fresh air might do you some good," Ophelia said with a small smile.

"Better thank you, you're right."

"So how come you suddenly went all pale and looked like you were going to throw up?"

"The stench from Toby's cologne."

Ophelia began to laugh at my answer. What was so funny? I wasn't joking. I smiled along and tried to contain my true feelings about how I wished I could pull out every one of those sparkling teeth, one by one, and rip out her tongue so she could never speak to Maximillian or anyone else ever again.

"Yeah," I said laughingly while looking at the ground.

"So, which way do you live?" I asked innocently. We stood on the road that ran by the studios. She turned her head to the left, and I caught a whiff of her watermelon and coconut shampoo.

"Just down this road and then to the right" she answered swiftly, while raising her left arm pointing in the direction of her house. I was damned that I lived the opposite way.

"Ah, okay, I live this way." I made the same gestures as she had done mere moments ago, only in the opposite direction.

"Cool."

"It's really not," I laughed. She smiled back at me. In any other instance, we would have said goodbye and gone our separate ways, yet none of us moved except a bit toward each other. She had the power of sending me into an unwilling trance, and I once again thought about how good it felt to smash her head against the floorboards. Her beautiful curls infected with blood.

"Well, I hope you get home safe and take care. Try not to throw up." The last sentence was said with a smile while she looked me deep in the eyes and stroked my arm. I had never experienced anything like this before, except from Toby, but he doesn't count. He's a man.

"Th-thanks" I managed to get out before I quickly turned on my heels and walked home faster than I ever had before. I felt her eyes boring into the back of my head as I walked away.

I didn't see Ophelia for a while after that, but right now, she wasn't my goal. Maximillian needed to be taken down a notch. As I walked into the studio a few days later, I tried to be as focused as I could without Ophelia interrupting my every thought. I went through 4 of the 5 main positions. However, when I began the 5th position, I caught a glimpse of myself in the mirror, and my world stood still. On my left side was Ophelia's body with Mother's face. She was laughing at me degradingly, and when she suddenly stopped and began shaking her head, I flinched and messed up the 5th main position. I had never made a mistake like that in my life, and the embarrassment of having to begin from the top once again was unbearable.

When rehearsal was done that night, my rage fueled both my mind and body. I needed to talk to Maximillian. I needed to know if my suspicions were true or false. Was he really in a relationship with Ophelia? My Ophelia?

Luckily, I ran into Toby on one of their breaks.

"Hey!" I said, happier than I usually was towards him.

"Hey," He was surprised by my mood, given how we parted the last time.

"I just want to say thank you for your help the other day, and it meant a lot to have someone there that I know and trust." While I spoke the last part, I recreated Ophelia's movements and threw in an eye flutter and hair toss now that I was at it. I know it was a bit much, but with Toby, that was all it took. And I needed him. He was my way in.

"Oh…err…, yeah, of course. Anytime. It was my pleasure." He bowed and had a hand on his chest while he closed his eyes and smiled stupidly. I wanted to roll my eyes so far back into my head that I would be able to see my brain, but I resisted the urge and decided that laughing lightly was probably more appropriate in this situation. At least if I wanted what he could give me.

"You know, I wanted to say thanks to Maximillian, too. I mean, for giving me space and letting me walk his girlfriend out, you know. Do you know where he is?"

"Yeah, um, I think he's getting water from the fountain."

"Thank you," I gave him a kiss on the cheek. "you're a darling," I said with a broad smile and turned away from a stunned and red-faced Toby.

I wasn't on my way to say anything to Maximillian. All I wanted was confirmation that they had an intimate relationship, and clearly, that was the case. I was standing in the doorway looking at the ballet mistress, attempting to get everyone's attention. Ophelia was nowhere to be seen, however, in the corner closest to the door was a very familiar pink bag. The kind of bag I would never forget. The top was open, and perfume, glasses, and her phone were sticking out. I was lucky I had changed into my jeans, as I then were able to slip the perfume from her bag into my back pocket. Everyone was too focused on the ballet Mistress, who made an example of some girl, to notice anything I did.

Chapter 10

The day was finally here. I was going to visit the Colley's Dance Studio. I sat in my room putting the slightest amount of make up on and, of course, a spritz of Ophelia's perfume. I was ready. I had my backpack with all the necessities and the cleaning outfit on. It was going to work. I could feel it.

I know that I technically did not have to get to her grandmother now that she and I had made contact, but just for the fun of it, I would be setting a few traps when I was in the building.

I had researched which cleaning company they used at the site. It was called *All Day Cleaning* with a little sun next to the last letter. I had spent all night sewing it into one of my blue dresses, and it looked perfect now. I said goodbye to Baryshnikov and off I went. I had the address in my invaluable black book, and it wasn't far away, only a 20-minute walk. As I was walking, I saw Maximillian on his bicycle. We waved awkwardly to each other as he passed me with a little smile. I saw him go down the road and to the right. The exact way Ophelia described when she told me which way she lived. I hated him. I hated her. I wanted to chop off his hands so he could never touch her again, and I wanted to skin her alive so that she would be forever cleansed of his touch. However, this train of thought had to wait for another time as I had more important things to tend to at the moment.

As I walked up the stairs in the building, I was met with a dusty smell. The cleaning scam had worked perfectly on the security guard they had hired two weeks ago. Because he was new, it was even easier to get by him, as he didn't know everybody. If anybody asks, my name was Claire.

I walked into a magnificent studio on the second floor. It had a reception desk and hangers next to the door where the children could hang their bags and jackets. To the left there was the first studio. Big mirrors on the back wall along with two beams. One in the middle of the room and the other one nearest to the mirror. After I took in the place, I opened my backpack and took out my hammer and nails and got to work. I put single nails in the floorboards, in the walls, and a few small ones in the beams. I knew they would probably be taken out before anybody got hurt, but just the thought of one of those nails piercing through the skin of Ophelia's grandmother or a child, was exhilarating enough.

I left the studio with a broad smile on my face. I nodded goodbye to the security guy (Garrett) and began walking back home, victoriously.

When I opened the door to my apartment, I was met with the sight of Mother. The last person I wanted to see at this moment, as I then wouldn't be able to continue my research and dwell in my recent victory.

"Hello dear, aren't you going to say hello to your mother?" she asked as she stretched out her arms for a hug. I didn't respond, only put down my bag, as silently as I could, and hugged her back slightly.

"What on earth are you wearing?"

"That's none of your concern, Mother"

"Would you like some tea?" I was dying for my nighttime cup of tea.

"Oh, now she can be polite. Yes, thank you, dear." She proceeded to go into the living room and sit down.

I went into the kitchen.

"So, what are you going to do about you not getting the part? I mean, you must have done something wrong!" She yelled at me from the living room while rearranging my pillows. Baryshnikov was nowhere to be seen. Such a man.

I pretended I hadn't heard her and focused on what I could gain from this encounter. I needed to ask about Aunt Tessa.

"I don't really feel like talking about it," I said as I placed the two cups on the table in front of the sofa.

"However, Mother, I did want to talk to you about something."

"No, no, dear we need to talk about you. We need to break it down and figure out how you can get-"

"I DO NOT want to talk about it!" I said as I stood up, and for the first time in my life, I looked down at Mother and raised my voice to her. It felt amazing, and I was excited to exploit the upper hand I had gained.

"I need to talk to you about Aunt Tessa," I said while I quietly sat down and folded my hands in my lap.

"All right, when you talk to your Mother like that, it must be important," she said in a disbelieving tone.

I sighed. "Okay, so what is the institution called where she is hospitalized?" I opened my black book and began writing it down, the second she spoke.

Mother finally left after a long night, and I had written everything about Aunt Tessa: her Paranoid Schizophrenia, her medications, and of course, the address of the institution. The next time I had a day off I would visit her.

Chapter 11

I decided that I would get into Ophelia's house. As I walked to the Studio, I was, once again, met with the sight of Toby as I left my apartment. This time, he didn't act as if he took a different route, he was deliberately waiting for me, leaning on his bike with two to-go coffees in his hands.

"Good morning, Sunshine" He smiled like an absolute moron.

"Good morning," I answered in a monotone voice, not returning his smile. I immediately regretted the way I acted the last time I saw him. And his attempt to be funny was just pathetic. How on earth would that be funny?

"I brought you a coffee." He lifted one of the cups in the air in my direction with a smile.

"Thanks," I accepted the coffee with a hidden gratefulness.

We began walking, and Toby dragged his bike with one hand and held his coffee in the other. We were back to our old routine of him talking most of the time, and me simply nodding and chiming in with the occasional yes or no. Even though it was only a 10-minute walk from my apartment, it felt like it went on forever, and I was still in wonder about how Toby could continue to have something to say.

All I wanted was to go into my own world that opened whenever I danced, and afterward, I wanted to find Ophelia and follow her home. I just hoped that Maximillian wouldn't interrupt my plans.

I don't recall anything Toby said from the moment he parked his bike, and we went our separate ways inside.

I went to my safe space, the rehearsal studio, and put my things in the corner like always. I admired my body and the gracefulness it executed the exercises in. After we were done for the night, I waited outside Ophelia's studio. Apparently, it was an early night for them, as it only took about 30 minutes for them to finish up.

I hid behind the wall that ran between the hallway and the bathrooms. I had always hated public bathrooms. You could hear every single bowel movement that went on in there, and because of that, I had vowed to never use any other bathroom than my own.

My heart skipped a beat when I laid eyes on Ophelia. From my hiding spot, I saw that she was holding hands with Maximillian. I wanted to retch. It made me sick to see and think of the two of them together. Luckily, they parted ways with the tiniest peck on each other's lips. I could feel the blood draining from my head at that sight. Maximillian looked like he was headed for a group of boys. I hated him for dating Ophelia, but I also hated him for not appreciating her every second of every day he had her. However, this meant that Ophelia had to walk home alone. Well, almost alone.

I waited for a few moments after she left, to continue after her. I did not want her to have any suspicions of anyone following her. As I began to walk and follow the exact route she had taken, I felt my pulse rise. I could feel the excitement all the way into my fingertips. It was pounding louder than it ever had before.

Because of the late snow that year, I could see the footsteps of her boots, even though she had already turned left toward her home. I followed the footsteps carefully and turned left at the main road. There she was. I saw her big, white, puffy jacket, the slender legs in tight jeans, the big winter boots, and, of course, her signature ponytail that hung down her back. Even from behind and a few meters between us, she was beautiful. I walked slowly, but still made sure not to lose sight of her.

She disappeared down the road, to the right, just like she explained to me a week before. As she was out of sight, I picked up the pace. Until I rounded the corner, it was good that I did, because it meant that I caught Ophelia opening the door to the third house on the right side of the street. After she had walked inside, I stood in front of the house and took it all in. It was a big white (possibly newly renovated) house with a balcony on the first floor. It was the kind of house I wish I had grown up in. It looked like the family inside would be happy. Before I got too sentimental, I turned around toward my own apartment.

The following Friday, I had to call in sick. I hated every morsel in my body for doing it, but it was necessary for me to complete the next part of my plan. I had written in big capital letters ENTER HER HOME in the black book. I intended to do so, but it had to be a time when she and her family wouldn't be home. Therefore, this Friday, I had to compromise. Because I had never called in sick before in my entire career, they were incredibly understanding, and I thanked Mother for giving me the gift of manipulation. I loved bending people to my own will. It was almost too easy, but I didn't mind. I did not need an extra challenge that day.

When I followed Ophelia home, I noticed where she had put her spare key after unlocking the door. It was under the potted plant to the left of the door when you had gone up the stairs. Morons. Anyone would be able to find it. But I smiled and hummed to myself all morning, as I got ready. I dressed in plenty of clothes to look a bit bigger than I was, in case someone might steal a glance of what was going on. I would take no chances. This was way too important.

I began walking down the street, and they were completely vacated (as I had predicted). I remembered to wait until the worst morning traffic had died down before venturing outside. When I reached Ophelia's home, the pounding in my chest began again. It was exhilarating, and I had a hard time containing my excitement. I walked carefully up the stairs that were made of stone, so as not to fall, and when I reached the top, I reached for the potted plant as nonchalantly as I could. Between the ground and the pot, was the key to my invasion. As I held the key between my hands, I remembered that there was no turning back now.

I put the key in the door and turned it around with a steady hand. It was happening.

As I opened the door, Ophelia's smell overtook me. As I took it in, I closed my eyes and dwelled in it before closing the door. I knew they didn't have animals, otherwise I would have taken different precautions.

A small hallway stretched out in front of me, and on the left side a staircase led up to the second floor. I decided to explore the first floor before venturing upstairs. As I walked through the hallway, I found a living room on my right side. I walked through the room and drew my fingers over the windowsills that pointed to the house next door. I ran my fingers over the sofa pillows, the cupboards, the coffee table, and the walls. I could feel the control rush over me. The frustrating feeling, I had had, was slowly disappearing the closer I got to Ophelia. As I turned the last corner of the living room, I was met with a vision of the biggest kitchen I had ever seen. It was in all white except for the handles on the cupboards that were silver. The floor went from the carpet in the living room to black and white squares in the kitchen. I ran my hand across the kitchen counter and opened all the cupboards in search for a glass. I found it on the third try. I crossed the room to the refrigerator and grabbed the orange juice in the refrigerator door. I poured a glass and brought it with me through the rest of the house. I turned the corner at the end of the kitchen and was faced with the door I originally had entered through. The staircase was now in front of me. Before I went up the stairs, I saw a door at the end of a tiny hallway. Curiosity brought me to it, and I opened it to find a bathroom. A big bathtub took up most of the space, and of course, I had to look through the cabinets but sadly found nothing of interest. Afterward, I went upstairs. I took my time, felt every step, and got to know them. A bunch of rooms met me when I reached the top. The first was a child's room with a ball on the floor, I picked it up and planted it in what I assumed was the master bedroom. The room itself was huge, and a king size bed took up most of the space apart from two dressers, a mirror, and two bedside tables, one on each side of the bed. I placed the ball at the foot of the bed.

The next room was what I had been looking for all along. It was clear that Ophelia was younger than me, and much less mature. I didn't even have to enter the room to find out that her dream was to dance professionally and make a living from it. On the door was a picture of dancers of the Russian ballet, and I couldn't help but laugh to myself at the thought of her talking and dreaming about reaching that level. She could never. I opened the door and was met with an alarming amount of pink. Even the goddamn curtains were pink! She had three photos on her dresser (also painted pink). One of herself dancing in the Nutcracker, which was all she had to show for her so-called career so far. The other two were of her brother and one of her parents. I placed all the pictures face down on the dresser, just so she knew that I now had the upper hand. In her open notebook, I wrote *Did you miss me?* as I hadn't seen her since I followed her home. I placed the now empty glass next to the note. I wanted her to know someone had been in here, and that she was no longer in control of her own life. I could get in anywhere, and control everything. She wasn't safe anywhere.

The last door of the hallway was another bathroom. "Just grotesque…" I muttered to myself as I took in the room. It was smaller than the one I found downstairs; however, the cabinets were filled with personal hygiene materials and pills. I carefully took out the bottles one by one. The fourth bottle I held read:

OPHELIA COLLEY – SERTRALINE

Antidepressants. "tsk, pathetic, little, weak Ophelia." I said to myself with a small smile on my face as I put it back in the exact spot I had found it.

I made my way downstairs again and quickly grabbed my coat and put it on. After I opened the door, I took one last look around the entrance and closed and locked the door behind me. I walked home victoriously.

Chapter 12

After two weeks, I was still high on my success and decided to exploit my momentum by visiting my aunt on a Sunday that was coming up. We had the day off, and hopefully, I would get what I needed from the visit.

When Sunday arrived, I packed my things, including my black book, and went to the tram. It took about an hour to get there, as it was located in a small city called Newington in Oxfordshire. But it was all worth it. I had found out from my conversation with Mother that she had been smuggling in Fentanyl to support Aunt Tessa's drug habit. I always thought of drug use to be a sign of weakness. Just don't do it. How hard could that be?

However, I needed to get my hands on the Fentanyl in order to reach my eventual end goal. I had called a few days in advance so that the institution was prepared for my visit. They were ecstatic, as Tessa had never had any other visitors except for Mother once a month. Most of the nurses I talked to did not even know that she had a niece. I rolled my eyes while I plastered on a fake, happy, and polite voice, so as to make the best impression possible.

When I arrived, I was surprised to see that I could just walk in. No need for a visitation. Mother had failed to tell me Tessa had been moved to the open part of the hospital to try it out for a period of time. Given her drug use, I thought it was a bad idea, but I couldn't help feeling a bit proud that she had managed to hide it from the nurses and doctors. Apparently, manipulation ran in the family.

I knocked on the door to her room and quietly said hello.

"Hii, Auntie Tess?" I said in a sing-song voice as I opened the door and smiled.

"Hello dear! How nice to see you! It's been forever!" she came forward for a hug, and I had no choice but to return the gesture as I had never been cold to her before. It had been, and is, exhausting to be happy and polite all the time. I don't know how people do it. But I figured that I might need something from her someday, which was now, and I was happy that I was able to get as close to her as I could because of it.

We separated, but she kept holding on to my hands and had lights in her eyes when she met mine.

"Would you like some tea? You like herbal, right?"

"Yes, thank you, that would be lovely," I said with a tight squeeze of her hands and a fake smile I sent her way.

"Alrighty, I'll be back in a minute."

She left the room, which gave me a bit of time to look around. It was a bigger room than I had expected, and there were a lot of bags and one cupboard under a sink. The window was locked from the inside, and she did not have a private bathroom. This limited my options as to where she could have hidden the Fentanyl. I bent my knees to face the cupboard. It probably wasn't in there, but I had to be sure. Before I could open it, I heard the door begin to open, and I stood up so fast that my head felt dizzy. I had never been more grateful for a warm cup of tea.

"Here you go," she said and handed me one of the cups. "So, tell me, what's new with you, sweetheart?" she asked nasally. I always despised the way she talked, and I hated that she didn't just call me Catherine. And I didn't know how to answer her question. I couldn't exactly tell her about Ophelia and that the entire point of my visit was to steal Fentanyl to kill someone.

"I'm fine, thank you. How are you?" I answered.

The conversation took its natural course. She told me about her hallucinations, voices, and how the government was out to get her so that we couldn't talk too loudly. When I had been there for about 40 minutes she had to go to the bathroom. I was excited to get a good look around and needed her to leave and stay away for a while.

As soon as she left and closed the door, I sprung up from my chair and went straight to the cupboard. When I opened it, I was met with a bunch of different creams, a hairbrush, a toothbrush, a pink bottle, I didn't know what it was, as well as three different shampoos and two conditioners. I thought it was a crazy number of personal products in the tiny cupboard until I remembered that she basically lived at the hospital, and it then made a lot more sense. There was only one shelf.

"Okay, one shelf. If I was Fentanyl, where would I be?" I muttered to myself. I began to remove some of the things and look around. Suddenly, in the very back, hidden under cotton balls, I saw two bottles with a clear fluid inside. They were small, but I knew that it didn't take much to kill a person with Fentanyl — especially if they were young and in shape. I had done my research as usual. I audibly gasped and smiled broadly at how smoothly everything had gone. I quickly grabbed the two bottles and put everything back in its place exactly as I had found it. I quickly returned to my chair, and as I heard footsteps coming closer on the other side of the door, I panicked and put the two bottles into my jacket pocket. Luckily, I thought further than to simply put it into my jeans pocket where the bulge from the bottles would be way too visible.

As the door creaked open, I quickly sat down, attempting to get my breath under control and not to make it too obvious that I had been stressed the last few seconds.

"Well, dear, I'm not allowed visitors to stay for longer than an hour, so I'm afraid I'll have to ask you to leave again," she told me sadly while looking apologetically at the floor.

"Of course, I should probably also get going – rehearsals are calling," I said with a small smile and a polite laugh.

"Yes, of course! Well, it was so nice to see you. Please come again soon."

"I will do my best, I promise," I said, with no intention of keeping that promise. I got what I came for, and I no longer needed a weak, stupid drug addict in my life.

Chapter 13

The weather began to get warmer. April was peeking out through the trees, and so was the slow but steady rise in temperature throughout London. Because of this, Baryshnikov spent more time outside sunbathing in the early morning as well as afternoon, sun on the balcony. I knew that he liked to play outside, catch mice, or do whatever it was that cats did. I just never thought it would end with him dying.

Some guy had apparently run him over by accident. Stupid cat. It was his own fault, and it happened right outside the apartment. I guess I had to bury him now? No, that was too much work for a member of the male species. I settled for throwing out all his things, as well as his body, in a trash bag and put it next to the containers in the back of the building.

Afterward, I got ready for rehearsals. I warmed up at home as I did not have the energy for Toby, and hopefully, I wouldn't have to talk to him.

I almost made it to the studio without running into him, but only almost.

"Hey, I saw you coming," he said. "How have you been? It's been a while since I saw you." He was smiling like the pathetic moron he was.

"I've been fine. My cat died, so I guess that's news."

"What?! Oh god, I'm so sorry! How did it happen?" Toby exclaimed louder than I would have liked.

"Is that really important?"

"I guess not." He said in a lower tone of voice while looking embarrassed for asking.

The small pause that followed was excruciating. "Well, bye," I said, with a neutral smile and a small wave, as I walked toward my own rehearsal studio.

I honestly did not care about Baryshnikov. He was just a cat; I don't understand why everyone made such a fuss about animals dying. It was his own fault.

The day went amazingly, and I didn't want to stop once it was over. Instead, I took a small break with a few stretches, some music, and water. Afterward, I danced by myself. I chose to practice my audition piece once again. Mother's words kept ringing in my head. *You must have done something wrong.*

I kept a watchful eye on myself throughout everything; however, in the last pirouette, I saw Mother's face in the mirror, staring back at me. It seemed as if time had stopped. I suddenly couldn't move unless Mother corrected my stance. I was in a trance and had lost control once again.

Ophelia walked in and brought me back to reality.

"Ah!" I exclaimed as I saw her. She was leaning up against the doorway, still in her dancing clothes.

"Sorry, I didn't mean to scare you," she laughed and walked toward me. My heart began to pound.

"What were you practicing?"

"Oh, nothing really. It was my audition piece." I mumbled to the floor.

"Well, it looked really good," she said as she adjusted the strap of her bag on her shoulder.

It did not look good. It looked amazing. I knew it, and so did she.

"How's it going with your team?" I asked after a brief pause, and a few awkward smiles had been exchanged.

"It's going great! Max is wonderful, but he's having a bit of trouble with his opening solo."

"Oh, I thought he'd been practicing for a while now."

"Yeah, but he has been mostly focused on the parts we dance together."

"Ah, I see," I answered.

An awkward pause followed while Ophelia and I stared at each other and the floor.

"I'm really sorry to hear about your cat. I lost my dog a few years ago, and it just completely broke my heart."

"Thanks," I answered in a monotone voice. Colder than how I previously had responded to her questions and comments.

Nothing further was said as I just continued dancing. I didn't understand the emotional attachment people had with their pets and did not need to inquire further.

When I got home, I immediately went in and sat in my purple chair. It was one of the only pops of color in the room, and it made me think of Ophelia's pink room. It was completely overdone, but mine was just as it should be. Cold and comfortable.

I opened my computer and did not even bother to make my tea or take off my shoes. I went into Ophelia's Facebook page and scrolled down to two years ago. I needed to know what kind of dog she had, what its name was, and how its head would look on a stick. Through brief perusing, I found what I was looking for. A tribute post to her stupid, fat dog. And its name was Baryshnikov.

I couldn't believe it. How could someone so untalented and unprecise in her movements be inspired by the same person as someone like me? It made no sense. If she loved him so much, she should have paid more attention in class. This was another sign for me to hurt her. Make her suffer like she had made me suffer.

Chapter 14

When I met Toby at my front door a few mornings after my realisation with Ophelia's dog, something felt different. He seemed even happier, somehow as if that was possible.

"Hello, you," he said unusually chipper.

"Hi," I answered hesitantly.

As we began to walk, there wasn't the usual line of questioning I had to endure, as he, this time, went straight to the point.

"Listen, I'm sorry I came on so strong that day with your cat and all that."

"Oh, yeah, sure, it's okay," I said, taken aback by his bluntness.

"But I actually wanted to ask you something."

"Okay…" I said hesitantly.

"I've been thinking about this for a while. It's really hard for me to ask, so please just let me get through it before you say anything, okay?"

"Okay."

"I really like you. And I think you like me too, and I would love it if you would do me the honor of becoming my girlfriend." He took a deep breath in and waited in anticipation. His eyes fixed on me.

We had now made it to the front of the Royal Ballet, and Toby parked his bike while I stood and pretended to think about how to formulate my answer. Of course, I did not want to be his girlfriend. The thought alone made me want to vomit, although it is understandable that he feels the way he feels about me. I am pretty unforgettable.

"Um, listen, Toby, I-"

"No, no…if the answer doesn't come to you immediately, then don't say anything. I know it's not what I want to hear."

He was right, and I was grateful that I didn't have to explain myself any further. We simply parted ways with a courteous nod and didn't see each other again until the opening night of our production of Swan Lake.

All through rehearsals, my mind was on what Toby had said earlier. It made me frustrated and mad instead of all warm and fuzzy like you see in the movies. The audacity he had when telling me this! If I had been anyone else, it would have put me in an impossible position. And when I really thought about it, he was being selfish. It was just because he knew I liked Baryshnikov (the cat) much more than I would ever like Toby. Just because my cat had died, he thought he could swoop in and become involved with me? God, what a child.

He had to pay for it. I would figure out how after the day was done.

As I was walking home, I noticed Toby's own cat wandering around. At first, I didn't pay it any mind until the idea hit me. I picked it up and cursed as it scratched me raw. I was happy it was going to die.

I took him inside, put him in the kitchen, and closed the door, while I found the hammer I had used in Colley's Dance Studio. I walked back into the kitchen and fought to capture the cat once again. I hit its head once to knock it out and make it stop scratching and fighting to get away. I then put it down on the tiles of my kitchen and smashed what was left of its skull. It was dead. Satisfied with my work and the message it sent, I cleaned myself up, put the body in a plastic bag, and put it into my backpack. I then made my way to Toby's apartment.

I knew that the close ensemble wouldn't be done for at least another 30 minutes, so if I wanted to do it, it had to be done now.

When I got there, I pulled out the bloody bag and threw it in front of Toby's front door. I had a key made to his building without him knowing, in case I needed it for something in the future. And at that moment, I was glad that I did. He wanted my cat dead, and I am simply returning the favor.

A few days went by, and the "dead cat" story was all over the studios. I couldn't help but smile at my own theatrical finesse.

It had been a long day, and all I really wanted to do was go home, stretch, and research more on Ophelia's life. However, just as I thought of her, she was, once again, standing at the door, waiting for me to appear.

"Hey," she said casually. "I need to ask you a favor."

"Going straight to the point, are we? No need to talk about the weather?" I asked jokingly.

"Nah, I know it's better to get straight to the point with you," she answered swiftly.

I smiled in response.

"So, what can I do for you?" I asked as we were walking. She tried to keep up with me.

"Can you please talk to Max? He is good, but I need him to be great. I saw what you practiced the other day, and it was brilliant! You could be just the right person to help him."

"Sure, but if he needs help, why isn't he asking me?"

"Well…he's shy, and I think he's kind of intimidated by you," she said this with an insecure laugh and a crooked smile.

I hesitated a bit before answering. "Fine, if he asks me, I'll do it."

"Yay!! Thank you!" she said while clapping her hands, jumping up and down, and going in for a hug. I put up a hand to refuse it.

After Maximillian managed to seek me out to ask for my help, I couldn't help feeling like I had a ball of bubbles inside me. This was my way in. It could not be more perfect.

Chapter 15

The first rehearsal took place a week after I had the excruciatingly awkward conversation with Maximillian. He had slowly gone up to me, as if he was afraid he would disturb me. As he was walking, I saw him in the reflection of the mirror and thought to myself that he would always interrupt my life, no matter when he decided it was a good time for him to talk to me. As we talked, I only half listened to what he said, as my mind was mostly focused on the way that I would end his life.

As I walked home, I decided to shelf my research on Ophelia and focus on Maximillian. My plan needed to be bulletproof, and even though I doubted I would find anything I didn't know, I still needed to be sure.

I took my time when I walked through the door. Luckily, I no longer had a needy cat to attend to.

I took off my coat, scarf, and shoes and placed my bag in its usual spot next to my couch. I made my way to the kitchen, and as the water boiled, I went to the bathroom, put on Ophelia's perfume, and relished in the thought of how not only my theft of it, but everything else, had also gone according to plan. This was proof that no one was better than me at anything. Whatever others thought they could do, I could do it better.

I went back to the kitchen and made my tea. I warmed my hands on the cup as I walked to the living room, which had begun to look like a cluttered office filled with papers and notes taking up all the space surrounding my purple chair. I began my brief research on Maximillian, but it didn't take long for me to get an overview. There was nothing to find that I didn't already know about him. He had two brothers, and his parents were divorced. Nothing of interest, except that he had changed his profile picture to one of him and Ophelia holding hands on a beach somewhere. The anger rose in me once again. How dare he?! He had no right to spend so much time with her and then show it to the world. She was mine and only mine. I was taken back to the first time I saw them dance. How his hands had access to every inch of her body, and I hated him for it. Because of how he underappreciated Ophelia, how he had touched her, kissed her, and been with her, he had to die. And the lovely side bonus was that by killing Maximillian, I hurt Ophelia as well.

However, this could not be like any other murder. It needed to be elegant and theatrical. I needed the world to know he was dead. How? I had no idea…yet.

It was clear during our first rehearsal that Maximillian was incredibly mediocre. He said that he was afraid that Toby (who was supposed to be the supporting role) would outshine him. I politely (however, falsely) told him he did not need to worry. Although he did, he did need to worry. Toby had never been amazing, but he was better than Maximillian would ever be. But if I wanted to continue our close relationship and have access to him, I needed to remain calm, happy, and supportive. It was unbelievable how weak men are and how much affirmation they needed all the time.

As I walked home, I mentally prepared for my night-time plans.

I was in my chair, staring at the two bottles of clean fluids I had stolen from my aunt. It was exciting. I couldn't wait to execute the plan that popped into my head as I focused on the bottles and papers floating around me.

Chapter 16

Three months later, summer had made its official arrival in England. There was no longer any need for big winter jackets and boots. I began to grow impatient for opening night, even though it was still a month away. It wasn't about the production as much as the reaction of everyone when my plan would unfold.

It was simple enough. I had gotten close to him during our rehearsals, tapping into how I used to act around Toby when we were still on speaking terms. It was almost too easy. I still didn't know if he was aware that it was me who had killed his cat, but I liked to think that he was. But that was neither here nor there. I had more important things to tend to.

Let me break it down for you:

The fentanyl that I had stolen from my Aunt was crucial to the first step. Maximillian and I had planned to rehearse together one last time two days before the opening night. I had deliberately chosen to move from the studios to the main stage.

Then, I would pretend to be concerned about him not drinking enough water. Little would he know that I was slowly putting more and more Fentanyl in his water, and at last, it would be enough to kill him.

I would drag him upstairs behind the stage and put a noose around his neck.

I knew that my plan required a lot of preparation, but I was patient and willing to play the long game.

At one of our last rehearsals, I decided to ask him about his relationship with Ophelia. I needed to know what he would say about her without any chance of her overhearing it.

He began to ramble on and on about her even before my sentence was finished, but I hated how it was all physical features he mentioned before her mind and soul – such a typical response from a man. For every word he said, I became more sure of my decision. There was no longer any need for him to stay alive.

As he was dancing, I saw about a thousand mistakes, but I had tried earlier to correct him with no luck. Therefore, I decided not to try anymore. I helped him as much as I could, but I could see that he had reached all the potential he had. It wasn't good enough for me, but apparently, it was good enough for the Royal Ballet. Typical.

I continued, however, with "helping" him to ensure that we would rehearse together on the last day of his life. It was thrilling to know that only I knew when that would be. I was in control, and I loved it.

When I came home, I made the last few preparations for the big day. I researched Fentanyl and Maximillian's weakest points. He loved his brother, as far as I could see, but I did not have time to get to him before killing Maximillian. And I, of course, had to remember to remain focused on my main goal: to hurt Ophelia and make her suffer.

Now, all that remained was to wait.

Chapter 17

Two days before opening night. The day was finally here. I made sure to remain calm and not show anyone that there was something out of the ordinary about this day. I went about my morning, even though I awoke earlier than I normally would. But today, nothing could kill my mood even if I saw Toby. Luckily, I didn't, and I was 30 minutes ahead of schedule and utilized this time to check that I had everything I needed, and then I warmed up longer than necessary when I got to my studio. I hadn't seen Toby in a while, but I guess he was mourning his cat. I laughed to myself at the thought.

The day went by more slowly than I would have liked. It had come together beautifully, and we had begun to rehearse on the mainstage, everyone together, after separate warm-up routines. It was a bit crowded on the main stage, but I was still taken back to the first time I went to the ballet when I was 9 years old. I was terribly angry that I didn't get to play the Swan Princess, and I was excited that the entire Royal Ballet, and especially, Ophelia would find out what would happen if they crossed me. I was not playing around.

Even though I loved being on stage, I hated the fact that I had been reduced to a wallflower, and after 15 minutes of rehearsing, I began to look forward to when it would be over for the day. I couldn't find the normal calmness in my dancing as I had been able to before, and it made me restless. It made me anxious to get out of there and find Maximillian.

When I found him, he had lights in his eyes and was on a natural high from our rehearsal. We exchanged pleasantries as well as I could manage. Luckily, I had had many years of practice in falsely being polite. We waited till everyone had left, and it was just the two of us together. He wanted to talk, but I wanted to get straight to the point. I interrupted him and told him to take it from the top while I filled up our now-empty water bottles. As his back was turned, I took his bottle along with mine, as well as one of the Fentanyl bottles. The sound of his shoes hitting the floor became more and more faint as I moved around backstage. I found the water cooler and screwed off the top of the small glass bottle with the beautifully clear liquid. I could feel the excitement churning in my chest as I put half of the bottle into Maximillian's water. I shook it and returned to the side of the stage as nonchalantly as I could muster.

An hour went by before he had drunk all his water, and I once again had to go and fill it up. As I was back at the water fountain and putting the other half of the fentanyl bottle into his water, I suddenly heard the door opening. I hadn't seen what time it was, and I'm guessing the janitors hadn't gotten the message that it was occupied. If I was caught now, everything would fall apart. Quickly, I closed his water bottle and jammed the empty glass bottle into my shoe. I quickly went to the door and told the janitor aggressively that he needed to leave. He looked at me apologetically, and nobody disturbed us for the rest of the night.

We had one day off before the dress rehearsal the night before the opening. Therefore, I allowed myself to push Maximillian as far as he could go. I needed time for the fentanyl to do its job.

When I returned, he said that he was getting a bit dizzy and tired and asked for his water. I gladly gave it to him. I knew that the dizzier and out of it he became, the more fentanyl I could put in his bottle. It was working. It was all going to work.

As the night went on, I put more and more Fentanyl in his water, and suddenly, he fell to the floor after a pathetic attempt at a pirouette. He had drunk two bottles of Fentanyl within a very short time and looked lifeless on the floor. He was still breathing, however shallowly.

"Well," I began as I walked in a circle around his body on the floor, grateful that I had locked every single door to the main stage. "This is it, Maximillian. God, I really don't like your name. It sounds so arrogant." I paused. "And speaking of arrogant," I said as I pulled a lump of his hair in my fist and forced him to face me, even though he was unconscious. I needed to tell him what he had done and why I did what I did. "in all the time I have known you, and even just known of you, you have been a pain in my ass and an arrogant son of a bitch. I can't believe you thought you could treat Ophelia and me the way you did without paying the price for it." I aggressively let go of his head, and he once again fell to the floor.

I paused again. I crouched down and began to whisper in his ear. "You're going to die. Not only because you took Ophelia from me, but because I need to get to her through you." I let out a small laugh as I stood back up. "And no one is going to know that it was me." As I said the last part, his breathing stopped. I kicked him softly to make sure he was dead. Even if he weren't dead yet, he would be when they found him.

They don't tell you how heavy a dead human body is. It looks easy when someone moves a body on film, but in reality, it is incredibly hard and takes a long time. I busted my ass for two hours, dragging his body up the stairs behind the curtain. It was a staircase with slim balconies on different levels which were made for the crew to stand on and pull different strings to make the set dance around with us. I had always been fascinated by the mechanics of how the stage worked, and now I would put my own personal spin on it.

As I crawled and dragged the body with me to the top of the stairs backstage, I had to take a break and catch my breath before I continued. What I stood on now was the balcony at the top of the stairs. At the other end, I saw the huge moon the graphics team had made. It was supposed to fly down in the middle of Maximillian's solo. Well, his understudy's solo.

Determined, I picked up his body and began to drag him by his arms towards the moon while I grunted and began to sweat. I found a loose part of the rope that I picked up on my way to the plastic moon. I threw it over my shoulder and dragged the body the last few metres. I sat down for a second and looked at his body. He looked so weak. Finally, his outside mirrored his insides. Weak and stupid.

I got up, made a noose with the loose piece of rope I had over my shoulder, and put it around his throat and neck. I couldn't keep myself from touching his neck and collarbones briefly before throwing him down on the planks. I tied the other end of the rope to the line connected to the top of the moon.

I left him there.

Afterwards, I crawled down, quickly grabbed my things, and left the studio. I was excited for opening night and to see the look on everybody's faces when it all would play out.

Chapter 18

Maximillian was missing. Nobody had heard from him (obviously), and I played along and copied everyone else's reactions and facial expressions. I couldn't help but smile for myself whenever I was alone. Everything worked! I was satisfied with my work, and as the moon was used in the first scene, I couldn't wait for everyone's gasps and general reactions.

Opening night was finally here. We were all in costume and waiting for the curtain to go up. The dress rehearsal went fine with Maximillian's understudy. Everybody asked everybody about Maximillian, and whenever I was asked, I simply plastered on an unknowing and confused face and lifted my hands so they were near my ears as I said, "I don't know. I haven't seen him."

Of course, everyone asked me, as I was the last person to see him, but I just played dumb. That's what everybody else would have done, too. But now, we were all getting into our starting positions as we heard the audience who had finally settled into their seats.

The music began to play, and applause filled the room before everything went quiet. The quiet before the storm. Only I knew it would all explode in a second. The understudy began to move slightly while the moon came into view. The cast were the last to notice the body hanging from the neck in front of the shining, silver, plastic moon. A small smile escaped for a millisecond on my face until the reality dawned on the audience, and a woman screamed. Everybody began to move and gasp, almost in unison. It was beautiful. "Oh my god, is that a body?!" a young woman from the seats exclaimed. I gasped along with everyone else as I saw everyone taking in my masterpiece. The curtain came down again swiftly, and everyone was pushed outside in a wild panic. The cast went out through the back, and the audience was let out the same way they had come inside. Over the speakers, a guy announced that the show was canceled due to a technical error and refunds could be applied for on the website. They were ushered out, and the employees attempted to keep the panic level at a minimum.

A technical error. The disrespect for my work was incredible. I hated them all.

I went to try to find Ophelia, and hopefully, she was devastated.

I found her in her dressing room, looking like panic had overtaken her completely. I tried to comfort her, but that was not exactly my strong suit. She thanked me for being there for her and told me that she was scared that it was Maximillian, as he hadn't been seen for a few days. I tried to tell her that I was sure it wasn't, and there probably was a logical explanation for why this person killed themselves.

It was so satisfying, lying about this. Until Ophelia suddenly said that someone should call the police. I knew that the police's involvement was inevitable, yet I didn't want her to think about that. I just needed her to be broken and never be able to recover. I just told her that I was sure somebody already did and stroked her back while she finally broke down and cried. It was music to my ears.

The police arrived not long after Ophelia and I left her dressing room. They had been told that I was the last person to see him alive and that they would like a word. I had prepared for this. I was not afraid. We went outside after I changed into my normal clothes. They assured me it was only routine questions, and they informed me that the body had been identified as Maximillian. I acted as surprised as I could and began to cry and look like I was completely broken up about the news. The officers tried to comfort me and told me that even though it was hard, they needed to ask me some questions. I told them that we had practiced two days ago and that he had stayed behind after I had left. They told me thank you for my cooperation and said that they were sorry for my loss. I thanked them and went inside, fake tears streaming down my face.

Ophelia found me again and asked if I was okay, with red and puffy eyes. I told her that the police had identified the body as Maximillian, which caused her to burst into a whole new level of brokenness, and I pretended to cry beside her. I thought she kind of overdid it, but I was glad that I had succeeded. Now, maybe, she would learn not to take what was rightfully mine or let anyone else touch her. Ever.

Four days later, I had the news on. Since our opening night, the news had only been running stories on Maximillian's death. I thought it was way too much attention for a stupid man. He had just died; it was not that big a deal. At the bottom of the screen, it read "DANCER'S DEATH RULED A SUICIDE" while the journalists talked indistinctly. I was humming happily to myself as I sat down in my purple chair with my cup of herbal tea. While I warmed my hands on the sides of the cup, I smiled to myself about my success.

Chapter 19

10 years have now passed, and I know that this letter has found its way to you, my dear Ophelia. You may have read this and are thinking about why. Why did I leave this letter to you? Well, I have decided to leave this world. I got away with everything, and as you know, I also got to dance as the Swan Princess. But you never did.

However, you may know this, or you may not, but I broke my ankle two days ago. I have been told it is a complicated break, and I won't be able to dance again. Therefore, I have nothing left to live for. I achieved everything I ever wanted, and now, I leave you with this letter. Maybe it got a bit out of hand (lengthwise), but I am not sorry. I am not sorry for killing your boyfriend. I am not sorry for going into your house, and I am not sorry for the thoughts about what I would love to do to you. Next to you, you will find the perfume I stole all those years ago. I felt that the least I could do was give it back, along with an explanation of what actually happened that day 10 years ago. You have been played. I played you the entire time we knew each other, and I am happy to tell you I got the last word. You do not control me. I control myself, and everyone who comes into contact with me. I have proved that.

I win.

Chapter 20

Ophelia sat back up and looked at the letter like it was poisonous. She put it back down on the table as if it were a bomb that would explode if she put it down too fast. She got up from the chair, her entire body trembling from the shock and anger that arose in her. Not only had she been deceived by Catherine, but she realized now that she had had no idea of who she had been and what actually had been going on in her twisted mind. As Ophelia attempted to regain control of her body, the TV screen in the background tuned her back to reality. It was the news.

"Ballet dancer Catherine Langley was found dead this morning. Authorities informed us that she died by suicide. This shows greatly how no one can truly know what the people around you struggle with. She will be missed by us all."

The voice screeched from the TV, and it felt as if Ophelia's entire world was working in slow motion. If what Catherine had said in the letter about her suicide was true, her confession to the murder of Maximillian had to be true as well. She felt herself begin to sweat and tremble. All these years had been a lie, and her entire career had been destroyed by someone who had no regard for anyone but herself. She was angry. It was clear that Catherine wanted credit for the murder after her death, but Ophelia was filled with hatred, frustration, and the feeling of needing to avenge her beloved Maximillian, who was taken from the world too soon.

Ophelia sat back down in her chair in the kitchen. The TV and any other sounds were blocked from her consciousness. She did not notice her phone ringing and vibrating violently on the kitchen counter, nor did she notice the birds singing in the early morning hours. Everything had gone quiet. She was fixated on how the chair felt underneath her. It was like a steady ground keeping her from falling through the earth. She turned once again to the letter. The words screaming at her from the pages. She had stopped smoking a few years ago but had bought a new pack the day before. It was lying on the table, next to the letter and the half-full bottle. She lit a cigarette and let the smoke spread throughout her insides, hoping that she would become one with it. But that was never the case. The smoke always got back out into the world with each exhale. The letter was tormenting to look at. It entailed every answer that she had spent the majority of her adult life searching for. But it was not enough. Catherine had gotten away with everything she set her mind to all her life, and this would make everything come full circle for her. Ophelia could not allow that to happen. She took her lighter in her hand and admired the design as she took another puff of her cigarette. The red lines curled around the black lines in perfect harmony. It looked small in her hand. She thought how incredible it was that something so small could be the root of disasters. She decided to put this thought to good use. As the flame appeared when she pressed down on the plastic square on the lighter's right side, she put out her cigarette and exchanged it with the letter.

"I hope you burn and suffer for the rest of your days" " she said as she easily and gently held the right corner of the letter through the flame. She admired how the flames danced elegantly around the letters and ate the paper as if it were the easiest thing in the whole world. If only the flame knew what it was really burning.

As the letter disappeared in the fire, Ophelia found peace. She had gotten the answers she had spent most of her adult life looking for. She had gotten her ending. She would not allow Catherine the same pleasure.

www.ingramcontent.com/pod-product-compliance
Lightning Source LLC
Chambersburg PA
CBHW070450170726
48291CB00005B/1690